Beautifully

Cracked

Remnants from the Soul of a Poet

CLEA MCLEMORE

ISBN: 978-0-9961442-3-0 (paperback)
ISBN: 978-0-9961442-4-7 (eBook)

Library of Congress Control Number (LCCN) 2024913303

Beautifully Cracked: Remnants from the Soul of a Poet
Poetry Collection
Published in 2024 by Clea McLemore

Edited - by, E.M. McLemore
Cover Photo - Courtesy of Clea McLemore & Brittany Howard
Cover Design - Dare2CareComputers LLC

Inquiries & special discounts for bulk purchases can be made by contacting the publisher and author at:
books@CleaMcLemore.com

Visit the author online at:

CleaMcLemore.com
Facebook.com/CleaMcLemore
Instagram.com/TheCLMac

First Edition

Contents

———

i

————————

Part Two: UNBROKEN 45

————————

———————

Part Three: BEAUTIFUL 91

———————

iv

Clea | κλέος (Greek) | Translated: Kleos

- To Praise, Acclaim, Fame, Glory Flower
- Her Father's Renown, Glory of the Father
- That which is heard or spoken, to call

Author's Note:

We were not made to be weak. Many of us are cracked, yet still unbroken...

Imagine a family of four; grandmother, daughter, and granddaughters who dreamed of one day having a real vacation. Venturing off to a place that had only been seen on TV or gasped at in magazines. Time, chance, and preparation one day align, and the small family travels in the dead-of-night to catch a flight to this foreign, yet native, land. It is to the great island of Bar Harbor, Maine.

One long ride on the open highway, two planes, and a rental car later; they found themselves scurrying to explore this natural wonder of nature. A long narrow bridge connected the island to the mainland. It was winding, rugged and worth the toil. As they made their way into the small welcoming town, they noticed the seashore to their left with a quaint restaurant overlooking the ocean not far from view; it was picturesque. The small family did what any Mississippi family does when traveling the open road and running upon such a perfectly situated sight; they pull over onto the side of the road and take a closer inspection of their discovery.

The four of them carefully scatter the mazelike path peeping above the water's edge, that leads to where sand lives beside the sea. The grandmother's daughter, who has now become a woman, leads the pack; the smallest cub not too far behind. They both bend down to take in a closer look and find hundreds of pieces of seashells cloaking the restless sand. The young woman, said to herself, "I thought there would be more unbroken seashells, than there are broken." But this was not so...

And as the broken seashells, that still sent messages to the hearts of men, were gathered in clear plastic, zipped- and-locked bags; there was one seashell still partially stuck in the sand. It was different than the others. Cracked, but not broken or shattered into pieces. It stood out amongst all the others because of this inherited feature. Its story, I imagine, is as equally unique as it is beautiful. Although this seashell was now imperfect, uniqueness has increased its value; furthermore, the beauty of its depth is only just now truly being realized and revealed.

And that my friends, is what many of us are today: *Cracked. Unbroken. and Beautiful.*

Every person has a story to tell. This book is filled with them. And my earnest desire is that along these lines, you will find one of yours.

Clea McLemore

For Rita, Shirley, James Earl, Mae, LaQuita, & Lisa

I carry you in my heart,
what is death?

[is it not life]

Not even it,
can keep us apart

Helping others when you cannot help yourself,
is wisdom.

The understanding;
this act, in return,
helps one's self.

Part One

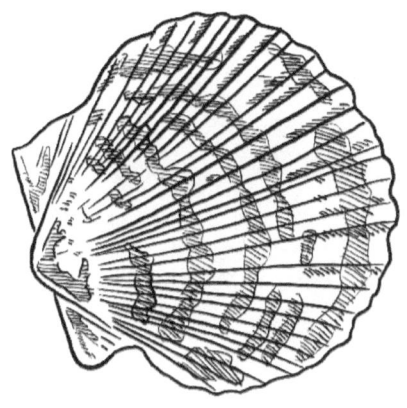

Cracked

Beautifully Cracked

I found-
a seashell.

Buried in sands
of time and pressure
yes,
it's cracked yet unbroken.
And there's true beauty
in that too.

Fight for Something

Life begins with a fight. As babies our natural reaction to being birthed is the need to breathe. Our little baby lungs fight for this barely noticed necessity, which is usually followed by crying and whining. Then, we fight to walk. Crawling helps to build leg muscles, but the legs are wobbly because the muscles have not yet been fully developed. But, wobbly legs still work.

Stumbling and falling become common occurrences; scrapes and bruises become proof that one has tried, and maybe even failed in the efforts to success. Yet, it is a fight to reach the next level of self-transportation: walking. However, the stumbles and tumbles prior to success are swiftly forgotten when one begins to travel on two feet alone.

Further down the road of growth, adolescence turns into teenage years; that's where you discover sweat, blood, and tears. Adulthood starts to beat down the doors between childhood and the age of accountability. It is an age we so frightfully strive to protect, but we soon realize that fighting is not a single action but a symphony of actions that create life's imperfect masterpiece.

Fighting must become a way of life. Because in order to live a life in this world, you're going to have to fight for it. There will be times when you want to drift onto the sidelines and give up the fight, settle for less because "Mr. Less" has become that unwelcomed friend, that ignores all signs of when it's time to leave.

However; settling on the notion that you are subjected to pressures of life that could never be improved, only stifles your journey before you have even begun. And, if you're going to fight for something, it may as well be your life...

Crack In the System

Crack
in the system.
Now family
broken wiiide open
drop-

Crack smoke, scattered scrambled yoke, lie
& choke on the truth
because it's too much to swallow.
Liquid spirits,
paper chasing,
hoes hasten,
hearts hallowed, broken

system failed.

Because it's run by people that surely do too.
The fabric of a torn nation
how do you think they will do you?

Head of Households missing in action. Rising taxes,
they don't insure abandoned neighborhoods
so discipline to youth gets fractioned
/education fractured/
which-soon-leads-to broken—bones
as folks run AWOL from their own broken---homes.

Fathers whipped, last names ripped, mothers chipped
family chopped---
We, so weak, it took minimal sweat
to sever the ties that bind us so closely together. Welfare,
public housing, food stamped, Medicaid:

that even paramedics...can't save
   families that don't know they need to be

We, legally black.
We, beautifully cracked.

After I Broke

You took time,
it paused.
So, you could place me
where my pieces used to be.

Pulled out the glue
and mended me back.
Now we can move forward
together, better
than ever.

Dangerous Verbs

The mouth of our posterity
wide open
their cries rise to the heavens
hoping
we'd fire and retire these
dangerous verbs.

"The Best Caramel Cake EveR:
To Big R & Shirley Mae"

"To the aunts who fed me neckbones, black eyed peas and cornbread; kept me in summertime and pressed my hair with heat like words press rhymes; to you have I inked these lines."

There is only one command to be executed,
one victory to be won at a time
one chance to devour that which is divine–
the eating of the Caramel cake is mine.

I touch,

     it crumbles.

Blessed are the hands that bake the cake,
the little sets of eager eyes that watch fantastic happenings
of white sugar, in a black cast iron skillet
when it boils with butter, under
the fire of an off whitish gas stove
being stirred until thick.

It is well
with my soul.

I loved you well,
I should have loved you better.
Now it's well after
the early ignorance of youth.
Well before those light bulb truths,
illiteracy isn't so bad when you have an orator,
I had you.

If only time had shown me just how tender

it would surely be
to me
and the aroma of those caramelized
Mississippi summers with you.

I would have made time make more
time for long-term
snapshots of clocks, they call
memories, and what I now call rhymes.

I recall holidays, when we gave God thanks;
gaze would slant towards your masterpiece
sitting off to the side, silently competing
between Shirley Mae's Lemon meringue and Sweet potato pies.
Truth is, I could never choose
but if today I was faced with the unforgiving choice,
hands down, I would choose-them-all.

Because, what is a Caramel cake without the baker?
What is Heaven with no Jesus?
What is a lemon or sweet potato Mississippi Delta pie without
its maker?

Taste buds drizzle, start to cry, and I
don't want to wipe the salivated tears,
when time took so many years
to taste the layers of love you left behind.

I find them still stuck
on the sides of most silver bowls.
On the tips of smiling children's sticky fingers.

Now I'm still stuck,
because I never imagined it. Never allowed imagine

11

to take me that far; imagination
present. You presently gone
now here we are.

What happened to you and I?
[you were mine]
When now, and here

         over there your body lies

in a stone-cold colored coffin.

Aim knows after hit;
life will never be the same.

All I have is now and pain
and hope and faith
that we'll see everyone
again,
I hope and pray
that is enough
for us.

Lord,
Thou art, so good
to me. Even when alone

I am not alone

Seize the Moments

You never know who you will meet, how they will affect your life, and who the people you encounter truly are or will become...

The year was 2018. There were two semesters left of graduate school and my studies would be complete. My major was Instructional Technology. All of my courses were in that field of study; however, I desired to have more instruction concerning something that did not align with my career or college major. I wanted to learn more about something that aligned directly with my heart. I yearned to take a poetry class for the pure pleasure, to further nurture my gift, and to improve my skillset as a poet.

I searched high and low; and behold! I discovered a course called "The Craft of Poetry" that was being offered for Master of Fine Arts (M.F.A.) students. Although I did not meet any of the minimum pre-requisites or requirements to take the course, I reached out to the instructor to see if she would make an exception.

The first answer went something like "Unfortunately you cannot, this course is for M.F.A., majors and you lack the requirements." But after sharing some of my poems, explaining how I would keep up with the curriculum, and making my case for poetry; she gave me a chance. This professor's name is Dr. Catherine Pierce. I passed the course with an A.

A few of the poems within this book were written in that course. Taking that leap of faith expanded my skillset, and it allowed me to tap into an area of writing that I had yet to experience. Dr. Pierce is now serving a four-year term as Mississippi's Poet Laureate.

Additionally, during that semester of coursework we studied a tantalizing poet, Ms. Joy Harjo. Her poetry was engaging, captivating, and encompassed a flair that is quite unique. The opportunity of time and chance presented itself, and Ms. Harjo scheduled a visit to campus for several days. Although I was unable to attend most of the events due to prior commitments, I was able to adjust my schedule and attend an editing session. During this session she helped me edit one poem, "The Best Caramel Cake EveR" was that poem.

Ms. Harjo would later go on to serve as the 23rd Poet Laureate of the United States for 2019-2022, one of two poets to serve a third term. She is also the first Native American, bestowed this honor.

A special thank you to Dr. Catherine Pierce and Ms. Joy Harjo for their feedback, instruction, and encouragement. Your guidance has continued to help me grow as a writer, and put into words, that which I yearn to put into words.

Seize the moments, take a chance, don't take no for an answer.
You never know what fruits or engaging encounters will sprout
from your leap of faith.

No Do Overs

Turn back
only to recall
how far you've come,
yesterdays
can't become undone.

Peeling Back Layers

He wasn't
ruined to the core.
There were just layers
she had to unfold
before she could
warm the place where
his heart was cold.

Now, she's cold.

Nature

The basic laws of nature constitute that for every action, there is an equal and opposite reaction. We as people are not eliminated from this universal surety. We tell our friends and loved ones to do whatever it is that makes them happy. What a dangerous dose of venom to give to someone you love or deeply care about.

Do we not consider that the very things that make us happy momentarily, could be the very things that haunt us for decades to come?

Bastard Child

But if any provide not for his own, and specially for those of his own house,
he hath denied the faith, and is worse than an infidel.
I Timothy 5:8, KJV

It was easy for him
to find a reason
to leave because,
he wasn't even there
in the first place.
His heart was with
his new life,
the new wife.

New almost picture-perfect family-
while his other child
was just a bastard
left behind
like grains of rice that didn't find their way
out the pot, onto a spoon.
Like trails of unused black and brown colors;
now dripping, still
drip drop
down
sides of an old paint can.
Now partially rusted red. Rejected.
Pushed away, on a back shelf somewhere
left to mingle with lost things,
where dusty lives, where something
is nothing,
and loneliness gives more lonely.
Lingering down and lying

up, on tops of books
.........................partially completed
of unwanted wisdom, thus deleted. Back-

spaces; quivering, in dark places.[tightly tucked].

Stuck.
Somewhere along the road
to a "Childhood's End"
and adulthood's unfathomable begin.
Barely riding on broken-down backs,
trekking graveled tracks of broken-down dreams
Daddy,
don't you see?
Your child now has broken wings.

His birdsong has been replaced
with the music
that non-flying birds sing.

But the young warrior is relentless.
So, he flutters his wings relentlessly,
heart fixed: "Let me fly lest I die."
Hoping quiet cries will be heard
perhaps, yearnings observed.

So, he prays that
silent screams can still travel
refracting through barriers, penetrating
matter in order for sound to reach-
and pierce through,
the deaf shadows
of a fleeting father.

Spilling Ink

I spilled my emotions–
right there
at your feet and
you stepped over
the ink
that bled your name.

Now,
my pen is dry again.

I Pray It Comes

It was you too.
You too who cooked up dreams,
fried and steamed them in a black cast iron skillet.
Poured them onto a platter of matter,
but the truth didn't.
It boiled and broiled until
my heart did too, for you
I bubbled, on a burnt stove.
Until all my moisture
slowly seized into
fleeing vapors of condensation.
Accompanying other refugees
who flee to the nation of broken-hearts.

Are we all just wondering, hoping, and stumbling
into lost pieces of broken parts.
Even lost love is s
ARt.

But I wanted to paint a more desirable picture today.
I wanted to make colors play
paint a rainbow's ray.
But
sunshine has grown gone,

now the black must bleed way long

.

.

.

.

.

.

.
.
.
.
.
.
.
.
.
.
.
.
.
.
.
.
.
.
.
.
.
.
.
.

Down pages of paper,
letters must collide as they're swallowed
into the shadow of present shade.

I only wanted a little sun today,
I pray
it comes.

Cancerous

You cancer, I'm patient.

Tired.

Of waiting in rooms
where the waiting was not soon
and the living was lost, in lost letters because,
no one bothered to put lost-
letters together.

Lost like, words to the wise, when they
un-woke. Loss like "I wish I would have saids"
to the now-dead; un-spoke. Just like, these cries murky and muffled
choked in choked throats. Life is but a dream broke. Folk so woke
they still sleep even though they walking. This is how we living.
Where everybody knows your name, but no one is calling on
hospital phones, but bills. Jill's sitting over here ill and
he's ready to collect on past threats- thus *Present*
presently stays in bad debt. Good credit; bad
fast, borrowed minutes can't last, that's why
I'm stuck in this impatience. Hog-tied
to this impatient room. Because,
I keep lying for you.
Hoping, for more
time, now
I pay
for it
all.

Don't know how else to pay,
so I pray, then work-
so I work.

Tight hands tightly write wrongs with currency of lead,
or intangible ink, thought thinks
from wrong to rights.

Eyes blink to search the earth, gotta make these weary words worth
the work, hand in hand with this hurt. With hurt hands hurt
hurts. That's why I love, on these un-lovely letters, make
them bend and *lean* on lines,
I read in-between them-
they help me evaluate
the real between
the whys.

And I could only sit-
there. and brace myself to endure
the sudden invasion
of truth.

But,

if there was a cure
that crafted
a way out,
would one be willing to escape it?

Tips on How to do the Shoulder Lean

Seeing usually believes what's seen.

Hope the shoulders are ready
wonder if the brain told muscles to move (it did)
they do

Move. It is all a blessing
that shoulders have sockets.
There are so many things that need connecting
the 60watt bulb, the ether
netting the cord to the cable modem.
The apple to the lips of Eve,
the eyes that pad the vision
Internet of Things webs bring
the friends on face
face, books that we dare not to face, for real.
Life knocked hard, for some, of us.

For us; phone displays ain't fair
and folly rides on air
or dies on stuck Ferris wheels.
Where the music was too loud and proud so they stomped
on ears, to mimic the drums son.
"You wonder why their cries can't get help?
Well, deaf can't hear dear."

So, here's some sign for the language
for those that have fingers.
Some small, others somewhat fragile-
but they all can pour a guest some tea
each can hold a hand,
grab a piece of earth. Build a church

mud-by-brick-by-straw-by-stick.
Together, fold a shirt, pass a smile.
Give some blood,
take off the pressure.
Travel the lost long mile and respect her.

Collectively break bread with brothers
hauling it from plate to palate
from empty to stomach then full.
Compelling taste buds to say "Taste sweet"
to fingers. It's all about the way
they come together.
Clutching each other in arms,
when the other is weak
leaning on shoulders that connect them.

Stolen Breaths

You should ask my permission
when you breathe
those stolen breaths you take.

Out of Reach

I saw you before, my eyes
in a vision.
In need of help but
I was not able to reach–
across the seas of barriers that stood in our way.
I held them long
but arms couldn't help you that day.

I pray, God did.

The Reuniting of States

Look
at us. Lost
in a frost
of unforgiveness's
polar vortexes.
We are frozen across
lakes and states
once United, now
we are broken. Now
pliable due to springs
that bring the melting
upon frozen parts.

Caught Up

She placed a blindfold around
lingering lids
so she could not see
the ache
written across his face
when he discovered;
her heart
belonged to
another.

When I Fell

I fell hard.

Like splattered paint
carelessly splattered onto a carefully crafted canvas of what
I thought life would be for me.
But the painting changed when I fell for thee.

I became,
adolescent eagle. learned to fly.
Living high, up above towering trees, carefully
peering over a ledge, in a nest, on a temporary edge called home.

I fell,
as the brilliantly yellow gentle leaf of october,
rocking where wind rocks
swaying side to upside, to down
all in due time.
Willingly, knowingly, ready for a fall
with incremental decline, unsteady.
Like a football in shaky hands
during Super Bowl season, and

I fell, like the pencil that rolls off the side
of a wooden desk for what appears to be no reason.
In motion, but not writing just rolling
along.
Not knowing
if its deacceleration will be due to dwindling force
or a permanent fixture of matter
jolting the fall.

I fell,
so hard
earth cracked and quaked.
Buildings rumbled
from the ache of
hands that wish
to touch my face.

Battered Beasts

Black hounds
howl, and yowl
in caged frustration.
In efforts to release,
untamed spirits of
battered beasts.

A Well- Deserved Crown

Over the course of a few weeks my eldest and I intermittently discussed the state and position of the black woman.

History is a reliable witness that our trials are exceedingly great, and our tribulations stain the pages of the history of the world. From youth the very hair on our heads bend, break, extend, turn, tumble, twist, and tangle in combs made to pave a way through lush woods with hidden uncertainty. The skin we live in has been used against us to characterize our worth, to rank our value, and as a reason to separate us as cattle.

We have been groomed to satisfy the pleasures of others, our bodies have been bargained for and bid on as currencies; for men ranging from slaveowners to pimps and what we now consider "social media." We were left without a defense. And as many of our fathers left us fatherless, we wandered into the raging waters of love, without knowing how to swim.

We cried our tears in secret corners, while wiping the tears of our broken men who become broken fathers to our children. We wipe their tears too. We hustle, we work, we grind, we make dollars out of 15 cents happen, and are master improvisers when the food is low, and the fridge is scarce. We are the personification of strength, the voices of faith. Some of our men degrade us, betray us, and replace us after we help to elevate, uplift, and encourage them to accomplish their dreams;

34

and still we stand.

Largely unheard, grossly underpaid, often unnoticed, but we still balance the crown that we so rightly deserve. We will continue to rise. Above every obstacle, occasion, each discouragement, and fear; and fearlessly spread the exquisite love that propels the earth to continue to rotate on its very axis.

Living Arrangements of Children by Race/Ethnicity
U.S. Census Internet release date: November 2021

- More than half (51.2%) of all Black children lived with one parent in 2022, compared with about one in five (21.3%) of white children.

- Between 1970 and 2022, the proportion of children living with their mothers in single-parent households increased from 7.8% to 16.7% for white youth and from 29.5% to 45.6% for Black youth. For children of Hispanic ethnicity, the proportion living with their mother in single-parent households increased from 19.6% in 1980 to 24.5% in 2022.

Internet citation: OJJDP Statistical Briefing Book. Online. Available:
https://ojjdp.ojp.gov/statistical-briefing-book/population/faqs/qa01202.
Released on January 10, 2023

The Queen's Shadow

no one notices
when shadows cry-
like royalty weeping. trees dripping leaves
the branches. they don't cry out
or scream
they stand
still, in dim dark.
eyelids blink back, blink black
ink dripping.
blurring vision, intermittent
thoughts, drifting from mind-to-matter to mist.
letters leave like leaves leave trees and twist
loss leaves.
real wrangles with destiny,
aches intermittently break through. water
falls splashing down fat
back and black. earthen worn leather, that bends
to toughened to ever break. [it's been tested]
back extends, shadow sits up straight: [fully vested]
while she whispers and roars in silence.

a queen.
nevertheless.

Real Life

We live in a world full of people that are hurting. These people are the neighbors we don't know next door, the strangers we ignore in congested airports, or the family members that are a call away but are too far away to call. You never know when someone is on the brink of giving up; instead of being the one that pushes them over the edge, be the one that lends a helping hand; and encourages them to shine again.

Shimmering Moments on a New York City Sidewalk

Someone sleeps on this street, so
remember to tread lightly.
Shimmering moments
are left
on the sidewalk _ _ _
you wouldn't want to

    c

    r

h u s h;

   s

   h
Them dead.

I saw her. Once.
Twice. Thrice. Alone and afraid.

Shimmering,
for a moment. On a New York city sidewalk.
Like time did, for that moment;
she, was a monumental moment.
We stopped, while the world walked by.
Afterwards reflected, concluded, decided, agreed that- she
was an angel, the shimmer was really golden; and we were
the unawares

A Piece of Hell

Sometimes
a piece of hell,
is all one needs to
woo flaming feet.
To run,
into the arms of
a piece of Heaven.

Shattering Time

Time shatters
but the pieces remain
we call them memories
label them as yester years
but today-
today
we live.

Speak, Child

Return
though the world has hurt you some
look closer,
there are layers of loveliness within untold,
part those silenced lips lost soul.

Speak, child.
Speak.

Darkness

Darkness, why do you knock
so loudly next to the door
of those you call kin.
I am without another, life
before I could grieve the other loss
of life, you have negated another
love in life,
I hate you tonight.

Of all the see men have seen
no terror has been more
terrible than you. See, you're more
terrible than that, you're terribly true.

Men cannot escape
the inevitable clutch.
Nor can woman work
wonders to woo it away.
No dragon could spit fire
to put out flame's play.

I need to know what's true today.
I unsheathe my sword and explore
the B-I-B-L-E, that's the book for me.
I decipher the Word that holds
the secret of time,
and there I find
your shadow. Some place around the start
but at the start you were not.

You slithered somewhere
in, between truth or dare

failure and fair
folly and holly
trees with berries in gardens
chex-mixed amongst finer things.
Eve saw you, but didn't recognize
the guise of luscious lies,
they-are-not-to-die-for.

All we want to do is live.

Part Two

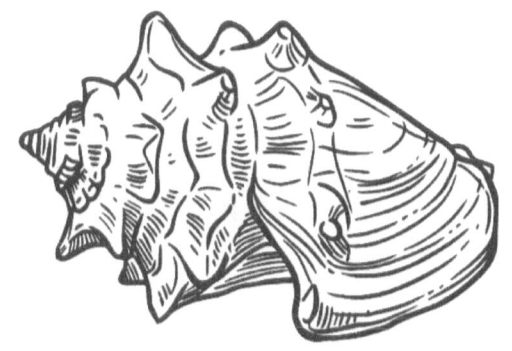

Unbroken

Natural Instinct

Natural instinct is to
expect nothing,
but I don't know what nothing is.
So I give it all and see what all will give.

The Contender

I am what a broken heart looks like. Remnants
of a whole blank face, faint with blushed red; an opaque stare.
Smoky mirrors smiling, with a spectacularly specular reflection
laterally inverted; hugging a silent prayer.
that is not silent.

The faulty coping mechanism: isolate heart and hide it,
(keep it tucked and quiet)
but the loudest thing about numbness is
its silence. The second, is the clinking of its cost.
If love don't cost a thing, why does free keep costing
me all these coppered colored pennies.

Wrath is cruel, and anger is outrageous;
but who is able to stand
before envy?

The friends are scarce, God is good, but the enemies
are plenty; most overtly friendly.
I'm talking today, but only those who
have an ear will hear me.
Let ears hear.

Because I am what a mending heart sounds like.
You can still hear each strand of thread carefully pulling
in optimism for the future,
despite needles sunk,
in the pinned cushions
of a pinched and pessimistic past.

I am what happens when you love
a love that could not last

past first lest last,
and my love is worth more than the sum
of all these things. In addition, I hold more
value than diamonds, rubies, or what a squirrel could bring;
but I'm no magician.

I am just the cracked clay that has enough
sense to stay on the Potter's wheel.
I'm the target of the enemy whose plan is to plot and kill.

But, if I'm the lion,
then tell me,
who's the meal?
If you put your
money against me,
and I'm the house;
then tell me, what's the deal?

I don't steal, but I do practice the war of arts,
of taking back what rightfully belongs to me.
If God said it, I'll stand on His Word.
His Word is bond, so bound by Word bond is free.

But my time ain't.

I am what out of time feels like.
Palpitating chests,
anxiety-filled time outs for cry,
but no time to cry out for rest.

I am the five more minutes you ask for in the mornings, but don't
have. I used to be the comings, now coming is going, some call me
"Don't Last." Yesterday has gone, today is a new day.
Present is now!

Now, present tenses past…Sun. Setting. Moon.
Darkness coats outside like a blanket bloomed.
Midnight, still bright. Now mid of night,
snake comes to bite but Son shines through,
like it's still mid-noon.
It only takes one push of the calf,
to walk towards forward and
light up dim rooms.

I am the glory flower
you didn't consider
that sees through the fright.

I am what you got me misidentified looks like.

Thou they try to bind hands and feet,
attempt to grind fine mind like meat
but like a stiff back's tightest muscle,
this soul will stay planted in this seat.

They thought, "We've won!"
One battle is temporal,
you can't defeat, un-beat.

Ask the snake, go rattle a tale
you never really knew your contender that well.

Push Through

In limbo.
Wedged tightly in-between
the person I used to be
and the person I will, be.
Today is the present, I have to live life. No what ifs,
or the roll of snake eyed dice.
The future is too real
to not get it right.

This present me,
wants to be free.

Caged birds have the tendency to catch cramped wings
creativity muffles in the mind of cracked things.
The unwelcomed visitor- complacency then
gets too comfortable lounging
in the stiff chair of life's, living room.
People's hopes die too soon
got to live now,
it's now after
noon.

Got to get through.
Each day is renewed-
and I'm too forward thinking
to live life in past times
when the present, presents itself so pleasantly
it's past time
so now I pass rhymes.

That refuse to live life bound in the same place
encaging the soul tempting grace.

That's why I stay laced up, so I can run this race.
Don't worry about the others, I just keep my pace.

Now I stare stories face-to-face
that are yearning to be said,
words pulling to be read.
And, I want to read them to you.
I want to break them down
piece by piece, moment by memory;
the perplexing state of life's complexities-
crush and feed them to you from silver spoons.
Until they become organic versifications,
then wash them down with spring and bloom.
All I have is truth for the nations
swaddled around this bitter, sweet
poetry. Not as pleasant as empty treats
but wrapped up tightly nicely and neat.

Rock it a little before I put it to sleep,
but even through unconsciousness
you can't silence a lamb
when it's time to speak:
no more than you can muzzle a preacher
when it's time to preach.
Get out the notebooks,
the poet is here it's time to teach.

I take the Word, hide it in heart
so when mouth spits, like roots, rhythmed, rhymes run wide and
deep; for some, wisdom is impossible to find
but I'm great at
hide and seek.

Like the Oak that stands

the trunk expands
to withstand
weight of these heavy hands.

The tree of life is quite ripe,
no serpent in light.
My God is God even in night,
without doubt I see sight.

That's what night visions are for.
Right?

Or, is that what night's visions restore?
Bright.

They told folk: dark equaled the sun wasn't shinning no more,
when earth was what was moving all along.

Light.
She writes…

Can't stop now.
Even if I wanted to,
don't know how.

Folks say "Give up!"
(Where dey' do that at?)
I know not how.
I'll just prove it-
no time like now…

So we push:
and get through -   -   -   >

Still Spilling Ink

Thought the well had run dry, so
eyes positioned themselves to cry,
but who knew this
ink would one day pen;
poetic prophecies again.

The Comedian

There's no way
I'm gonna die for your love.
I lied for your love
and lying wasn't enough?
Now you want my life too?
Funny you,
funny you.

Silent No More

She spoke
for the first time.
Her words fell
like rocks in a coal mine;
she picked up hammer
& a pen
promising to never be
silent again.

7 Minutes

Approximately seven minutes have passed,
you lost your virginity just that fast.
Your pores taste of his sweat, your made-up face
stained-down with child-like tears
your skin sticky and wet.
He's gone too quickly to console your fears
and you haven't even gotten up yet-
if you fear consequence,
you'll loathe regret.

Humidity-filled droplets of dread
encapsulate your body like a wall,
(have you feeling like a nut.)
Like it, you too were once whole.
But skating around with the nutcracker
will have your fruit cracked, broken
open youth drippling slowly to the floor, prematurely-
picked, pricked red with envy.
A little less shimmer, a little more dimmer within.

You made a bad move, now you
sinning against your own self.
And since sin can't win; you lose worked for
wages; inwardly poor, spiritually suicidal.
Your poor self-searching, amongst other poor selves
for the pearl you dropped; you spot an idol.

Now self-loathes,
to-and-fro, as pearl is tossed under hoofs of pigs, rolling
around in hurt dirt
beneath the stomach of mangy dogs and lingering and wagging
tails of time,

[that body gon' trail you
(like that stray you keep feeding) for a very long time]
but right now, you're out of it.

Every ride comes to a stop. And this
is where you get off.

In seven minutes, your innocence, your purity, your pride
have been too generously tossed to side.
It's too late for second guessing; guess the second's up,
just like it's too late to ask the guy for testing.

You went into unknown battlefields with no protection,
now you pray for better blessings,
and pray you better–
for lesser lessons.

And the irony is,
you didn't even want to.
You just did it because he said he loved you.
Because you didn't want him to go to,
another girl who,
would do the things you wouldn't do.

Tears become your next best friends, and you hate them all.
Since they have the tendency to fall, together, but still fall all alone.
While bitterness is too brittle to bite the truthful bullet
that stops the pumping of naïve hearts.
But, hearts are a phenomenal wonder
even when iced,
they can thaw out and beat again…

Woman of the Living God, pick up your crown.
Hold your head up, not down.

Make better plays next time, prove you're the MVP.
Queens are much more valuable running kingdoms alone
until they meet their kings,
than laying underneath a dog,
for 7 minutes.

Do not give dogs what is sacred; do not throw your pearls to pigs. If
you do, they may trample them under their feet, and turn and tear
you to pieces. -Matthew 7:6 NIV

We Fight

He wasn't defeated
will was depleted
rest was needed
momentarily-
It's midnight,
tonight we rest and pray
tomorrow,
we fight another day.

Nothing but the Truth

You wanted my lips
(closed)
in silence.

To appease
the possibility of causing offense.
But my throat
thrusts forth
truths–
even
for you.

Depression

Is such a dark and effective spirit. Because of it, marriages have ceased to exist, families have been relentlessly severed, and people that should be here with us are no longer present. It is not a term to be used loosely. Having a bad day is not depression. Depression is more like being in a dark bottomless pit of sorrow, looking up; but unable to see even a particle of light. It's going to sleep in order to not feel pain, only to wake up angry, because the new day holds the woes of yesterday.

But the interesting aspect of depression is that there is a way out, it's a climb. If you fall or are pushed into a hole surrounded by dirt, mud, and soil what would be the next step if no one was around to help you out of this predicament or hear your faint cries? You could look around and see if there were any logs that you could stand on. Check to see if there are any rocks sticking out of the dirt on the way up that would help you climb. Do you have a small blade that could help you start moving soil out of the way? Can you build a mound with the left-over soil? The answer to every one of these questions may be no, but they are useful because they eliminate the things that won't work to get you out of the hole, and they make room for you to explore more feasible solutions to your escape. But the fact remains you know you're in a hole, and you have to find a way out.

So, if you or someone you know is struggling with depression, things may not start looking up tomorrow or even next week. But each and every day you must seek solutions that will lead you to a personal excavation of pulling yourself out of the depression that has taken hold of your life. Take it back. Your life is yours, do your best to act like it: Every day you can. Find your why to push yourself to get up and get dressed when you don't have to. To read that book you need to get around to, to study for an exam that could change your life. Whether it's your faith in God, your family, your children, your creative works, or even your pet; find your reason to dig yourself out of the hole you stumbled into and live the life you were destined to live.

For I know the thoughts that I think toward you, saith the LORD, thoughts of peace, and not of evil, to give you an expected end. Then shall ye call upon me, and ye shall go and pray unto me, and I will hearken unto you. And ye shall seek me, and find me, when ye shall search for me with all your heart.

Jeremiah 29:11-13

When You Get Up

Heaven says, "Arise."
Creation replies, "But, this is my favorite chair."

I sit, it sinks, life stares
back stiff, still cares.
But even the familiar still falls
like premature promises that faint
down flat. This seat is no good
for bad backs, I get up
take one step forward
and back, back. Deep
is where I got stuck at.
When I couldn't do nothing,
when ground wasn't around,
when feet met no place to land.
I was in sand, but it was too quick
to hold in these hands;
I realized everything
was in God's plan.

This is my favorite chair.

It holds me and doesn't care
if hair is combed or what body has on.
It protects me from the bone cold floor.
But, I don't want it to no more.

Spirit must sit up and finish the fight
towards right, far away from
misguided folk.
If life is but a dream, you can find me woke
on the side of the bed.

Whispering my last goodbyes to the luxury
of living in ignorance. It, indeed was bliss
fully not. Because when facts entered the room;
the exit was too crowded with lies
for truth to get by
so, now I'm stuck with it.

Legs can't move, feet housed, in housed
shoes. Trying not to lose another foot,
or tip of toe, tipping in the wrong
direction. Balance is essential,
the use of limbs is such a blessing,
so is rest. So, I bless His Holy Name.
Take hands, hands touch,
palms. Arms reach, meet
towards Heaven. Soul thrusts up prayers and pray;
trying to hold on to the one soul
we all get, without selling or throwing it away.

"I am cold
as a shiver."

Skin feels chills,
chill bumps lift hair, held, in mid air
insides shake. Alive still,
on side I wake, and
thank God for another day.

Tick Tock, Drip Drop

…there goes time
slowly dripping.
No cusp of hand
can hold,
when its built to flow
over fingers
bend corners and wrap wrists
twist curves
take risks.

Take a breath and capture it
before the wind does.
Things can get lost
in wind.

Losing Battles

You didn't lose the war
this was just a battle
one fallen victory
you tried, you failed.
Now get back up
and go at it
again.

Confessions of a Guilty Man

I know I was wrong when I
picked all the cherries
from my neighbor's Cherry tree.
I left not one, cherry on the one tree
but it meant the world to me.

They were just dangling there
twinkling in Sun
red and proud
bright and round
and boldly
beautiful spheres
of pure Heaven.
I tried to stop after one bite,
but I looked up and I'd had seven.

Since seven is the number of completion,
you know I had to keep on eating.
Mind pulled back the reigns, told hands to "leave some"
but taste succumbed to the stubbornness of weakness
and left not one.

It was me against the sweetest of sweet treats.
Tingling buds of taste receptor cells
standing in the face of massive temptation.
If you only knew what I was facing…
I am but flesh Your Honor
merely a little lump of dirt, I know;
but it's the dirt that helps the cherry trees grow.

Did you know, I smelled them
and they smelled like life?

Ask dirt and soil.
They too saw them sprout
out of bark and limbs,
like arms out of tight sleaves;
fingers leaving impressions,
you should have seen those blessed leaves.
They twisted and sung
fell and hung
like lights of life
throughout my day dark night!

It made me believe in goodness again
in honesty, integrity…

Okay, Your Honor,
I confess to the crime.
I am one thousand percent guilty this time.

Still Standing

Your exit
left
me
barely standing;
however,
the muscles in my legs were
stronger than assumed.
I went right on
standing
like I used to.

Shining Scar

I was ashamed of
that mark
below my knee, a scar.
Painful to remember, yet
unbeknownst to me;
it would set one free
and be
my shining scar.

The Incredible Journey

So,
I look up at this mountain
high in sky-
this has happened all before.
I take wisdom and will
and begin to climb
one rock
one limb
one step at a time.

Higher

The dark night sparkles
because of the bejeweled sky.
Folks tell me to wish upon stars
but even they will die,
so I wish more high.
More miles in-between
more atmospheres
to get nigh,
to my Maker.
Looking for the place
where the real Hope lies;
 no forsakers.
Higher–
beyond the heavens…

Purpose

Whatever you do
do it great
do it wholly,
boldly
without apologies.
Without microphones
or whispering ears.
Do well,
even if no one hears.
People call
stuff like that
integrity.

Remember Spring

When the last leaves
of fall drift from weakening trees;
when white becomes cold
the young winter's old.
You may fail to remember many things,
but I implore you to;
remember spring.

Make You Proud

It's not just about
making you proud.
It's about
the joy received,
each time I achieved
what you always knew I could.

Believe

If birds can push
off invisible air;
and we can live from each
impalpable breath we breathe-
All is possible if we truly dare
to truly believe.

Observations of a Heart Doctor

Turkey Creek Jack Johnson: "Doc, you ought to be in bed.
What the hell you doin' this for anyway?"
Doc Holliday: "Wyatt Earp is my friend."

Turkey Creek Jack Johnson: "Hell, I got lots of friends."
Doc Holiday: "...I don't."

"Tombstone" excerpt, written by Kevin Jarre

Folks chanted your name,

      rose
you   to fame.

Then they cursed you

in the very self-same hour, same power.

They salted your skin,
fed your popped corn to loud hungry crowds;
but we all gotta eat now.
Thousands of screaming fans
congested within those, sodium filled stadiums.

Pressure went up in air. Doc Holiday said,
"I'm afraid the strain was more than he could bear."
Hands froze up, call *Dr. Cardiac,* heart just got arrested.
(You just wanted to play ball) You weren't ready to think of
a tombstone message.

They crammed your defeated valves;
bounced you.
Balled you up in baskets, hung you in white web

dunked your soul beating red.

Waited until you stumbled and rolled
so they could kick,
and
beat you
dead.

But that's impossible-

when you're not through living yet...

No Forgiveness for Honesty

I ask no forgiveness for honesty-
but, I'd rather be alone.
Where no man lives
fighting victories-
Fearing no man's fears;
than be surrounded by crowds
that blankly stare
into eyes of blissful ignorance and
yesterday's complacent mediocrity.

Value

Is simply what something is worth. A typical rock does not have a lot of worth. It is easily accessible to almost anyone, and costs zero dollars to acquire.

Pearls, however; although also naturally made, are not easily accessible and can cost thousands of dollars to acquire. If God has breathed the breath of life in you, then there is value in you because you were made in the image of God. The sooner we start to understand and live like we have value, the less we will allow others to treat us like mere rocks being kicked along the sidewalks.

But there went up a mist from the earth, and watered the whole face of the ground. And the Lord God formed man of the dust of the ground, and breathed into his nostrils the breath of life; and man became a living soul.

-Genesis 2:6-7

Value of a Pearl

Now that I know my value
you can't expect me to
cast these pearls before swine
so, before you rend me
I'll politely
decline.

After October, the ARt of Remembrance

Here we are, no more remembrance.
The goblins are gone, or are they?
Fall has fallen into the 11th hour of tinkering time.
We tinker with time, and name it remember.
Recollect, the timed ticks as they pull hours
out of cracked backs bent over,
toiling under the weight of nature's
hard, heavy hand. Living is work.

And the work is always worth it,
and, so much more, when living meets purpose.

An octopus has 3 hearts;
one for each beating season.
Spring beats nicely, summer beats hot,
fall beats sweetly, and winter can appear to beat
not. It's last, and first
and cold, and old and foggy
and causes living things to walk
through the valley of the shadow of death
but where there is a valley, if you look up, you'll see
there is a hill from which cometh help.
Lord come, Lord by, Lord here.

Because where the Savior is, there is indeed a testimony.
and for a testimony to stand you're going to need
an expert witness; we want to remit this.
So, subpoena, the substance of things you hoped for.
Gather all the evidence of things you have not seen,
walk towards that thing; and let your faith, make you whole.

This is the ding your stomach hears when
the turkey can come out the stove.
This is the only reason trees know
they're not dead when they're really froze.
This is why we wait patiently for spring to say,
"See? They still grow."

This is where the calloused hand greets the anticipated harvest,
why morning leaves and evening seeds
obligingly move in dark winds, to be
carried away, buried with an unseen
hand planted in wide fields and
sandy lands.

Under a thousand circling circled suns.

To start their journey
of thanks and giving, of seasons and living.

So. We. Live.

And for this and so much more,
we remember to say, thank You.

Surrender

Like metal
under an unforgiving furnace
I melt, I am now pliable
just right for moldability.
Each joint wills to give up the fight
and put up arms.
Tonight,
fingers extend like branches in Oak trees
Your Spirit a rushing wind upon evening leaves
I pray sin flees, as I yield to thee.

Night Vision

It was dark out.
The night thick and wet
heavy shadows covered me,
but the ship's eyes
could still see.

As I awaited the warmth
of morning.

Ode to Writers

It's lonely
on the edge
of mortality.
Ode to the sacrifice
from painters + artists
with brushes + pens
that encourage us, to win.

Tight Spaces

You were unwavering
during the best of times
but
more importantly
there
in-between places
tight spaces
no one else dared to
squeeze into.

Beautiful Remembrance

This illness, these void spaces, have no cure.
Those who loved and lived
now on the other side.
It hurts, it makes me afraid.
But I'm okay with
the ache of
beautiful remembrance.

Part Three

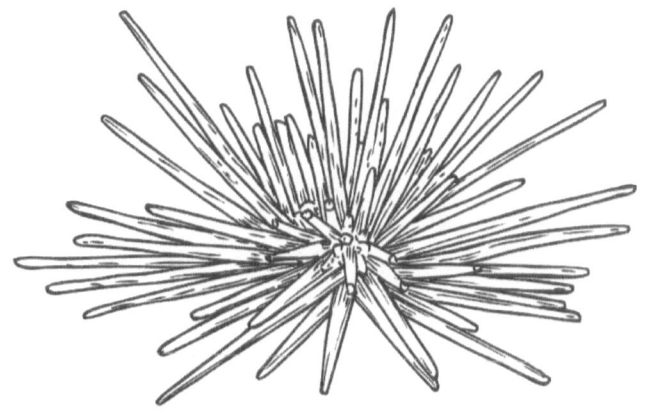

Beautiful

The Sea Tells Time

And God called the dry land Earth; and the gathering together of the
waters called He Seas: and God saw that it was good.
Genesis 1:10 KJV

It's not easy to be defined
when no container can hold me wholly.
Only when I am solid
am I still unmoving. melt, drip, glide

and gas up skies.   fowls only see me   when the clouds cry clear

they bid me to come float with them and their high-pitched groans
they don't even know my name
so they call me *Necessity.* Forget the food
who needs clothing when the wet doesn't have shelter.
I'm multi, but the creatures I protect have outlived dimensions

especially when places like land and masses
remain too self-serving to care for me; I wanted a bear hug, but they wouldn't
hold me. So I pushed them around their plates,
made them settle for a piece of crust.

I thirst.

Swallowing slimed creatures whole
and they live
and
drown
and fight for life, even though day is night
and centuries delicately wave decades goodbye.

I'm salty. My cousins and kin stay fresh

while I stay here housing the mortal creatures of forever
a little more
embracing the true beauty of a spotted mantle
as it encapsulates the flamingo tongued snail.

Even though I know those hog fish will
gobble them up, then go about the day.
The crabs claw at me,
the Coral reefs leave only crumbs behind.
As I orchestrate the rebuilding of life, seas-
we are good. Waves save days amidst gravity's pushing
currents while Sun glides; reflecting time's clanking lock
and tomorrow's too soon Moon.

Beautiful Symphony

The orchestra
plays melodies of
humbled hearts tonight.
A beautiful
symphony of aches
break through.
Leaving behind
only you.

Singing Scars

I see them-
marks once cut open
now carefully healing
although there are
no more open wounds
there are remnants of past tunes
giving you the blues
that's when I
get lost loving you
& start by
kissing your scars
away

Nothing's Forever

Nothing's forever
except
eternity
(& God).

Love in Autumn

I would love to love you like
autumn loves leaves
like sight loves to see
but what are all these musings worth
if thou does not me?

Slices of Life: Pains & Pleasures (A Villanelle)

You were the first you I ever discovered
I caught God's smile, held it a while; and I wept
You were a jewel I had to uncover.

I loved your cry before you knew I was mother
gave you my tears as you began your best quest
You were the first you I ever discovered.

The early bird chirped late, there was a stutter.
The weary worm wiggled, survived the test.
You were a jewel I had to uncover.

Two hearts walked a street one day, one beat the other
innocent apologized, guilty never confessed.
You were the first you I ever discovered.

I heard a bird flying, there it hovered
until something pushed it down for rest.
You were a jewel I had to uncover.

Love, I do not deserve you, there's more worthiness in others
I pray *Worthy* doesn't find out yet.
You were the first you I ever discovered

You were the jewel I finally uncovered.

Where I'm Going

I can't take you with me my darling,
you would not like it there.
Over there they get lost in books,
they get glued to the spines that hold
secret worlds together.
They fall in love forever,
over there.

Love of a Poet

You love a poet
a warrior of language.
I draw my inked sword for you.

Implacably strike through ~~words~~ that thought-
they would stay there on the paper f-o-r-e-v-e-r
I mourn for them.

Then betray them by
sprinkling unfamiliar nouns and verbs
amongst their feathers of letters.
Then run back later to realign them
in-tight-lines, that, didn't want to make you mine
but I'm a word slayer so they had no choice
but to get in line
so I could right the wrongs then re-write lines
and make them wait to
stand in line---
just to wait;
like I wait for you.

These are the things that poets do
when they love someone like you.

Love of a Poet: Part II

So,
as long as dust lives
there you will live
beating in this heart
whether both in present dwellings or continents apart
you beat with me
and God will give the increase
      between I and thee
We
are you and me.
Christ will make us,
just one.

One breath
on one wave of riding wind,
we'll drop off sin
make room for Truth to get in.
So he can be a witness to:
nothing but the truth.
I love you as I love myself
remember that;
when you're remembering how much I love you.

Like life
you live
and never die
then so will I,
so, will I.

On treble clefs and library bookshelves,
is where you'll find
the life of a poet.

Love of a Poet: Part III

Waiting.

To hold you like music holds
four beats ----
Now I'm a whole note beating
holding oval notes four times
on five lines,
four spaces,
endless rhymes.
On treble clefs is where you'll find me remember?
I'm music
I twist time.
Because in no time, time sees you.
I'm eyes,
in order to have vision I need you.
But you're air,
I can't live unless I breathe you.
And like water,
I'm for certain two hydrogen and one oxygen
are both needed to be you.
Your presence precedes you, and
I just want to be in it.
So we can show the world

what love is.

Take Me Away

JC I know You'll come for me
take me away
to Heavenly places,
then will my fingertips skip
along the lines of
Heavenly spaces.

My Devotion

I step beyond the water's edge
heart pulsating & pledge
devotion to Jesus Christ
lover of soul
lover of my life.

The Last Days of Summer

It's effortless to get lost
in the last days of summer.
I only need the thought of you,
(oh, there you are) right next to solitude.
Uncovering heavy covers that hide my hidden solace.
It's pointless, to try and find me, I'm lost in the last days of summer.
With you,
I'm un-alone. hoping the season does not end here. with me
alone. I'm searching for the secret space where
hearts hide. And found mine, deep
in the depth of your eyes.
Love is a wonder, so
it is no wonder,
but I wonder
why, you blink
and my soul
holds it,
like time

in a picture.

Still...

Wide Spaces, Not Far Enough

There are

these wide   spaces   between us.

Lonely lands,
crumbling masses
untamable seas.

But there is nothing nowhere
broad enough--------------------
no low land high enough
to keep you
away-from-me.

Man Down

There was a nice young man
who ran errands to town each day
no one could make him stay.
He ran so fast even light couldn't catch him,
he didn't know *Love* was going to test him.

One day *Hate* put up a bet,
that *Love* couldn't catch him because he hadn't caught him yet.
And *Love* didn't bet on much but if he did
on this young man, would he place his bid.
So *Love*, without a doubt in mind
knew that he would get this young runner in time.

He waited
for just the right night.
Called in a few favors and
under a moonlit night
saw
two feet pacing chasing
night's shadow
to avoid the arrows of Cupid
but the night shines as the day
….man down.

Life's Not Fair

This behooves me,
to think of why I'm yours.
Why God saw fit to piece
together the jigsaw puzzle
of my life and place you there.
Life's not fair and
neither is love-
but I'll take it.

Jealous

It's an empty nest,
at best,
when birds learn to fly
I-
now jealous from the air
that thrusts wings
to the free birds that sing.

Eighties Baby

Ice cold lemonade
for sweaty May,
honeysuckle drops and plastic broken flip-flops.
Window air conditioners, beaming sun-rays.
Mud-pies made after rainy days.
Frozen Kool-Aid and rocking chairs.
Whether hot or cool outside children play
under shaded Pecan trees
run, skip, dance and fall
in love with lovely leaves.
My generation
loves these
simple things,
we're 80's babies.

Linger Still

Oh love, won't you linger here a bit?
Recline in mind, exhale and sit
by fires well lit
with lyrics of time.
A heart full, could be fuller still
if I were thine.

Still Moments

Moments, have become troublesome
as they tussle to pass without you
round about you
like nights do.
Tiptoeing around Sun
ducking and dodging dawn
and the morning's dew,
but even grass can't get rid of you.

Moments in Time

Times like today,
the thought of you
passes still.
Still passing thrills,
thus, you linger…linger still.

Still Time

And I wonder
if indeed I did lose you,
could I find you again?

Back then
I couldn't love you as you deserved,
but wisdom is a dish well served.

Years have equipped me for such a task
to love you for however long love lasts,
and lasts, and lasts, and lasts
I hear,
it's forever...

Summertime

If love still breathes
love me like bees
do pollen on petals
in Mississippi summertime.
When I'm really alive,
but love me
better.

#SixWords

Your words
see me
like eyes.

No More Maze Runners

Running aimlessly
around a maze of denial,
when all I had to do
was run to You.
Finding refuge
under the Shadow of
your Almighty wings.

How to Draw a Dream

Here, we have the canvas of our lives
etched and carved with things old
and new and true.
We break, we mold, we mend, we make
now it's me and you.
Crafting imagination with our bare hands
making dreams come true.

Take the quill of my heart,
pair it with the brush of your soul
and I'll show you
how to draw a dream.

My Heart Waits

My heart waits.
Somewhere along
a worn long dusty road,
where flowers and caterpillars fight to bloom.
Where conquerors never give up
and desert the field too soon,
and the fighting Sun tangles
with winter Moon.

I'll be waiting for you-
still fighting
my soldier,
the love I stand beside.

You need not ever wonder
what or why
or where
I am.

As long as hearts
beat
yours will beat in mine
I carry you there.

And you move just like you are rhythm.
Rhythm
set free to
happy hopeful children.
Toe tips meet the dirt of their creation
brown puffed up clouds circle the beat
pulsating with each rise and fall
moving to music.

You my muse, my stroke of paint, moi très bien
like saints without sin, you, my very well.
The membranes of my soul's protection,
God's secret place of earthly perfection.

I'm willing, I want, I wait for you-
until young turns old
until ice heats up, melts again
then turns back cold.

Minutes with you
make seconds seem old,
times outlive lives and forevers.

Oh, that life would be good to me
and give me you forever!

But most love poems
don't last that long
they bend under time and their pressure,
read one that will last, ask Edgar.
Ask his Anabelle Lee
if the kingdom by the sea,
was all that it seemed to be.

I believe, so
be that to me.

Because those that don't know love
couldn't recite this song,
line for line, rhyme for climb;
it'd be too long,
they wouldn't have time.

But if you were a poet and loved someone like I love you;
you'd become a thief of night-
steal time. then write,
as many wrongs, as you can rights.

But tonight,
I write what's true,
a heart, that waits, sometimes
impatiently for you.

Ode, To a Japanese Magnolia

It begins in *spring*.

You were so patient.
Patient, like a Japanese Magnolia tree
who holds its flower,
even when other beauties
start to bloom.

It waits,
bearing wide deep green leaves.
This wonder of nature,
could easily be missed amongst;
a great Oak, or a large slender Pine.
It thrives, but the velvet jewel in it hides
[it is not time to bloom yet].

The welcoming *summer*
comes, Sun shines in all its glory,
giving energy to roses, lilies, lilacs, sunflowers, tulips and
the magnificent hydrangea.
Deep purples, charming blue hues; when I see a hydrangea
I always feel as if someone's told me good news; frown smiles.

But the journey of patience had only just begun;
you were as patient as the Morning Sun.
That waits through all the day,
just to steal a quick glimpse of the moon.
A moment sooner, would have been a moment too soon.

In *autumn* you brought colors,
into a life that once was filled with black and white.

In you, the sight that the eye does hold
held, gold; and hands held behold.

You must be a tree
because *winter* came and you were still there standing
with me.
The cold came, you were still standing
right there,
with me.

The wind stripped the few leaves
that were left from autumn's fall.
Time, was harsh to you
the drops of iced life hung from your weakening branches
its aim was to cool an already cooling heart,
snow and ice engulfed your trunk
wanted to freeze you to death–
But you weren't through
living yet.

Children walked along the sidewalks and paused
at the sight of your crackling branches.
Sometimes snowballs were even thrown at you;
the ice was too icy to feel the warmth of second chances.
As you shivered from the cold. coarse. rain
that dripped. and froze again.

Through it all, patience chose to endure
there was no sign of a tree bringing forth a flower,
but you've always had life in you;
you just bloom in a different season.

And just when nature thought it had run you off
with its beating rain, and high winds;

you did something few trees can ever do
right in-between *winter* and *spring*
you chose then to spread your wings.
Before the others got their chance to bring
out their best.

Like patience you bloom in tune.
Like a perfect symphony does right before
the director nods.
You could've tried to outshine others
but you waited instead.

If love is patient,
then you my dear are as patient as a picture can be, still.
Perfectly painted by perfectly deftly moving hands
that draws each. lovely. leaf.
That colors deep earth and sweetens the smell of souls,
you are what other flowers look up to behold
just like I do.

Ode, to a Japanese Magnolia.

Fame & Glory: Part II

Life chasing me
baiting me
making me question
poetic profession.
But I looked in the mirror at my story
and recalled
that it was all for
His Fame & Glory.

Epilogue

We were not made to be weak. Many of us are cracked, yet still unbroken...

...Although this seashell was now imperfect, uniqueness has increased its value; furthermore, the beauty of its depth is only just now truly being realized and revealed.

And that my friends, is what many of us are today:

Cracked. Unbroken. and Beautiful.

This is your story. You are the co-author, and God is the Author and Finisher of your faith. Write accordingly. ~Hebrews 12:2

Visit the Author

CleaMcLemore.com

Facebook.com/CleaMcLemore

Instagram.com/theCLMac

TikTok.com/theCLMac

author@CleaMcLemore.com

Notes and Reflections

Cracked: What challenge, setback, or obstacle in life changed you? How did these changes make you stronger?

_____

_____

_____

_____

_____

_____

_____

_____

_____

_____

_____

_____

_____

Unbroken: What event did you think would break you, but didn't? How have you used this event to help others?

_____

_____

_____

_____

_____

_____

_____

_____

_____

_____

_____

_____

_____

_____

Beautiful: Name one thing about your life that is beautiful. Explain why you chose this selection.

_____

_____

_____

_____

_____

_____

_____

_____

_____

_____

_____

_____